Too Much Space!

Read more of Beep and Bob's
adventures in space in Book 2:
Party Crashers

BEEP AND BOB

Too Much Space!

written and illustrated by Jonathan Roth

ALADDIN

New York London Toronto Sydney New Delhi

ALADDIN

An imprint of Simon & Schuster Children's Publishing Division
1230 Avenue of the Americas, New York, New York 10020
First Aladdin hardcover edition March 2018
Copyright © 2018 by Jonathan Roth
Also available in an Aladdin paperback edition.
All rights reserved, including the right of reproduction in whole or in part in any form.
ALADDIN and related logo are registered trademarks of Simon & Schuster, Inc.
For information about special discounts for bulk purchases, please contact
Simon & Schuster Special Sales at 1-866-506-1949 or business@simonandschuster.com.
The Simon & Schuster Speakers Bureau can bring authors to your live event. For more
information or to book an event contact the Simon & Schuster Speakers Bureau at
1-866-248-3049 or visit our website at www.simonspeakers.com.
Book designed by Nina Simoneaux
The illustrations for this book were rendered digitally.
The text of this book was set in Adobe Caslon Pro.
Manufactured in the United States of America 0218 FFG
2 4 6 8 10 9 7 5 3 1
Library of Congress Cataloging-in-Publication Data
Names: Roth, Jonathan, author, illustrator. Title: Too much space! / written and
illustrated by Jonathan Roth. Description: First Aladdin paperback edition. |
New York : Aladdin, 2018. | Series: Beep and Bob ; [1] | Summary: After being
humiliated while on a field trip to Pluto, Bob, with the help of his alien friend Beep,
tries to change his personality and overcome his fears (heights, darkness, space, and
spiders) before the next field trip to a black hole. Includes facts about Pluto.
Identifiers: LCCN 2017012320 | ISBN 9781481488525 (pbk) |
ISBN 9781481488532 (hc) | ISBN 9781481488549 (eBook)
Subjects: | CYAC: School field trip—Fiction. | Outer space—Fiction. | Human-alien
encounters—Fiction. | Fear—Fiction. | Schools—Fiction. | Science fiction.
Classification: LCC PZ7.1.R76 To 2018 | DDC [Fic]—dc23
LC record available at https://lccn.loc.gov/2017012320

For Lisa Marie

★ CONTENTS ★

Too Much Space!

SPLOG ENTRY #1
A Horrible Place Called Space

Dear Kids of the Past,

Hi. My name's Bob and I live and go to school in space. That's right, space. Pretty sporky, huh? I'm the new kid this year at Astro Elementary, the only school in orbit around one of the outer planets. There's just one micro little problem:

SPACE IS THE MOST TERRIFYING PLACE EVER!

If you've been to space, you know what I mean: It's dark, cold, airless—and it goes on for infinity! Okay, maybe it ends at some super huge wall. But what's behind that wall? More space? Bigger walls? Giant space *spiders*?!

Just kidding about that last one. There are no spiders in space.

Are there?

No really, are there?

Beep just said to say hi. Beep is a young alien who got separated from his 600 siblings when they

were playing hide-and-seek in some asteroid field. Then he floated around the void for a while, until he ended up here. Sad, huh?

You know what's even sadder? I was the one who found him knocking on our space station's air lock door and let him in. Now he thinks I'm his new mother!

On the bright side, everyone at school says Beep is super cute and fun to have around. And since he won't leave my side, they let him join my class as the school's first alien student. He's definitely a quick learner—he picks up languages in no time, and his grades are already better than mine!

Anyway, I'm writing these space logs (or splogs, as we call them) partly to tell you all about my hectic life, but mostly because it's an assignment to show you how "great" things are here in the future. At the end of each week I'll put all my entries into a time-velope and mail it to 200 years ago. If you receive this, please write back; and while you're at it, please also include a pile of vintage twenty-first-century comic books! Thanks.

Beep will help with the pictures. He's super talented and loves to draw, though in his excitement he sometimes eats all his pencils.

Hope you enjoy!

★★★★★

SPLOG ENTRY #2
Space Spiders!

Astro Elementary is a big space station orbiting Saturn. I think they picked Saturn because it looks cool in the brochures.

Trust me, I tried to get out of coming here. When I took the big admissions test, I filled out *C* for every answer. Instant fail, right?

Wrong! Turns out I was the only

kid on the planet this time to get a perfect score. Now everyone thinks I'm some kind of super space genius. I'm a failure even at failing! My parents were more surprised than anything, but as much as I begged, they wouldn't let me stay home *or* send my little sister in my place. She seemed particularly happy to see me go.

Beep and I share a dorm room in the living section of the station. Class starts promptly at 8:00 a.m., so we sleep in until about 7:55, then quickly float through the curved halls to our classroom. (Since there's no gravity in space, we have to float *every*where.)

Professor Zoome is our teacher. She begins each day by taking attendance.

"Zenith?" she called this morning.

"Here," Zenith said.

"Flash?"

"Here."

"Blaster?"

"Here."

(Everyone in my class has pretty cool space names.)

"Bob?"

"Here," I said. (Okay, so not *everyone*.)

When she was done, Professor Zoome clasped her hands together and said, "Class, I have some very good news. After you finish your morning splog entries, we're going on a field trip!"

This time last year, when I was still in school on Earth, we had a field trip where we went on a hayride. I love hayrides!

"To Pluto!" she added.

"Pluto?" I gulped. Pluto didn't have hayrides. It probably didn't even have ponies.

"No class has ever been on a field trip to Pluto before," Professor Zoome continued, "so it is very important to select a responsible partner. It should be someone you can share notes with, as well as someone who will risk life and limb to save you in any one of a billion probable space emergencies."

Double gulp.

Beep bounced up and down. "Pick Beep, Bob-mother!" he said. "Pick Beep!"

As if I had a choice.

"Okay, time to go," Professor Zoome said when we were done with our splogs a few minutes later. "Everyone to the Astrobus. Blastoff in five minutes!"

I don't know what Astrobuses were like in your time, but these days they're the pits. They smell like a mix of nuclear waste and peanut butter (and I'm allergic to peanuts).

"Beep call window!" Beep said as we floated aboard. I still wasn't used to all this floating, and it was definitely making me dizzy.

Once we had taken a seat, Beep pressed his face against the glass. "Saturn rings pretty," he said. "Go round and round and round and . . ."

Make that *very* dizzy.

I looked away, just in time to see my classmate Lani floating down the bus aisle. Lani is short for Laniakea Supercluster (which is a cluster of more than 100,000 galaxies, including ours). Not that I looked her up or anything. And even if I did, it was only because I wanted to learn more about her cool space name. Because I'm, you know, totally into everything about, uh, space.

Lani grabbed a handrail, coming to a stop.

"Hey, Zenith," she said to her partner, "let's sit by Beep and Bob!"

Zenith shrugged. "It's the only seat left anyway."

They settled in directly across the aisle. "Hey, Bob," Lani said. "How's it going?"

"Um. Um. Um . . ."

Before I could finish my thought, Beep popped up. "Why Bob-mother face so red? Too much hot in bus? Too much radioactive? Too much—"

I put my hand over his mouth.

Beep removed my hand and buckled his belt. "There yet?"

"We haven't left," I replied.

"Yet?" he said a second later.

"Pluto is billions of miles away, Beep. It'll take at least twenty minutes."

"Beep want snack."

Snacks happen to be a true passion of mine. Unfortunately, my stomach lurches about twelve different warp zones every time an Astrobus takes off. "In a minute," I said, trying not to hurl. Hurling in zero gravity is super unsporky.

The moment we leveled off, I scrolled through the Servo-server options on the seat back, but all they had left were orange-swirl ice pops and salt-free peanuts. I ordered an ice pop and it instantly shot up through a tube.

"Beep too!" Beep said. In seconds, his tongue was orange and the ice pop had disappeared. "Again!"

"We're only allowed to get one," I said. "Next time eat slower."

"Beep want next ice pop bigger!" he said.

"That's the only size they have."

He pouted for a moment, then leaned over me to stare at Lani, who was removing a jar from her backpack. The jar was buzzing.

"Snack?" Beep asked.

"Not for you, Beep," she said. "These are houseflies. For my latest science experiment."

"Huh?" Beep said.

Now that I was feeling better, I decided to play it cool and show Lani that maybe I was a smart astro guy after all. "Lani is obviously studying the controlled effects of zero gravity on tiny Earth insects that are used to flying in the confines of an atmosphere."

Pretty impressive, huh?

"Actually," Lani said, "the flies are only here to feed the subjects in my other jar: spiders."

(Note: those lines = me fainting.)

When I opened my eyes, Lani's face was spinning. Kind of like Saturn's rings. "What . . . what happened?" I said.

"You fainted when you saw my spiders," she said, holding them up again.

Okay, so maybe I had a slight fear of spiders. But she didn't have to keep shoving them in my face.

"Beep like spiders," Beep said.

Lani leaned forward. "Me too. They're actually my pets: Alpha, Beta, and Zilly. They're cute, friendly—unless you're a fly—and extremely smart. Look at their webs."

I peeked. The first two spiders had written complicated math equations. The third seemed more like an animal lover.

"They used to live in the ceiling of a lab where

there were lots of gamma blasts," Lani explained. "And I think the energy made them geniuses. That's how they can write messages like that. Though I don't always understand Zilly."

"Some pig!" Beep repeated.

"Some creepy insects," I corrected.

"Actually, spiders are arthropods," Lani went on, "of the order Araneae. There are tons of interesting things about them, such as—"

Luckily, Professor Zoome's voice boomed over the overhead speaker: "Prepare for landing," she said. "Dwarf planet approaching fast!"

SPLOG ENTRY #3
Ice Not Nice

Correction: *We* were the ones approaching fast. Though I guess Pluto was going fast too, in a relative way. In space everything goes fast.

The Astrobus landed with the normal amount of smoothness, which is equal to riding a triple cork-screw roller coaster inside of a giant blender on top of a free-falling elevator.

"Now, kids," Professor Zoome said, "Pluto may be

small and cute, but it's far from cuddly. Nearly all its surfaces are icy, and its atmosphere is a thin layer of silent but deadly gasses."

We all chuckled at that one.

"Furthermore, it is dark, cold, and you have an eighty-eight percent chance of getting hopelessly lost if you don't follow directions. Unfortunately, our Astrobus's air lock can only hold one student at a time. So who wants to leave the bus first?"

Wait, did she say 88 percent chance of getting lost? That only left a 22 percent chance of *not* getting lost! Or was it 11 percent? Or . . .

I started counting on my fingers. But, to my shock, instead of counting, my hand shot up.

"Thank you, Bob," Professor Zoome said. "That's very brave of you to volunteer."

"But . . . but . . . !" I said, trying to pull my hand down. That's when I realized it was being held up by Blaster, who was in the seat behind me. I finally yanked it free.

"Good luck, space wimp!" Blaster chuckled. His buddy Atom chuckled too.

Blaster, I should mention, kind of doesn't like me. I should also mention he's about the size of a small moon.

I sighed and stood up. I then grabbed a space suit and helmet from the rack in back and slowly made my way up front.

"Don't forget your Visor Light," Professor Zoome said when I was suited up.

"Check," I said.

"Or your Emergency Space Pack."

"Check."

"Or your Secret Astronaut Diaper Kit."

"Uh, check."

I opened the hatch and took a deep breath. "This is one small step for a kid," I said, "one giant leap for gaaaaaaaaaaaaaaaaaaaaaaaaaaaaaaaaaaaaaaaaaaaaaaah!"

"Most importantly, don't forget to switch out your Space Boots for Ice Boots!" she called.

Now she tells me!

I had stepped onto slick whitish-orange ice and was now sliding downhill at about a hundred miles per hour. Toward what? Who knows? Probably more ice!

I pretty much thought I was dead, until— miracle of miracles—my field trip partner popped up beside me, foot surfing the ice like a pro. "Beep go wheeeeeeeeeeeeeeeeeeeeeeeee!" he said.

The cool thing about Beep is that he adapts instantly to any environment, so he never has to wear space suits or anything (and I do mean *anything*— you think all that bluish rubbery stuff on his body is *clothes*?).

"*Help!*" I cried. But somehow he thought that meant "help me go faster," so he gave me a push.

Pluto has a small amount of gravity, but it wasn't nearly enough to slow me down. I sped farther and farther along, sliding up and down icy hills until I finally came to a stop at the bottom of a deep crater.

Beep did a perfect triple flip and landed on his feet. "Pluto fun! Beep go again?"

"I have a better idea," I said. "Get me out of here!"

Beep handed me my Ice Boots, which I put on. Once I

climbed to the top of the crater, I stopped to catch my breath. The bus was a yellow dot on the horizon.

Beep's eyes were wide. "Zowwie," he said. "Bob see what Beep see?"

I stared at the vast white and orange landscape. "Yeah—ice."

"Not ice." He began to bounce. "Ice *pop*!"

Leave it to Beep to turn the dwarfiest planet into the largest treat. He dove back into the crater and began licking its sides.

"Yum!" he slurped. "Taste like orange-swirl!"

"Are you serious?" I asked.

"Bob-mother try!"

"I think I'll pass."

"Enough for *both* Beep and Bob-mother."

"Enough for the whole galaxy," I said. "But I'll still pass."

He shrugged. "Suit self."

I waited for him to stop, but he showed no signs of slowing. And that's when it hit me: If Beep was right, and Pluto was edible, he had just made a major scientific discovery. And you know what a major new scientific discovery means?

"Money!" I cried. "Beep, you're incredible. We'll open the biggest ice pop stand in the solar system. We're going to be *rich*!"

Pluto suddenly wasn't looking so bad. In fact, it was starting to look quite tasty.

"Guess I'll try a little after all," I said with a smile. "You know, just to make sure."

Even with my space suit's special trademark GasAway! fan filter, I knew I could only open my visor for a few minutes before the fumes would knock me out and the cold would make an ice pop out of *me.* But I didn't need much time. Just enough for one little lick.

I slid back down into the crater to join him. "Okay, Beep. Here goes."

I popped open my visor.

And stuck out my tongue.

And licked the ice.

That's when I made two of the most horrific scientific discoveries in history:

One: Pluto does *not* taste like orange-swirl. Not even close. Beep had only thought it did because the ice was orange and—as I'd sadly forgotten—his taste-receptors are *in his eyes.* And,

Two: MY TONGUE WAS TOTALLY STUCK!!!!!!!!!!!!!!!!!!!!!!!!!!!

SPLOG ENTRY #4:
Hurts the Force Does

So there I was: tongue stuck to the ice. A deadly chill seeping into my bones. And a really terrible itch forming in that one little spot on my back I could never, ever reach!

Luckily, I had a field trip partner, sworn to save me in one of a billion probable space emergencies.

Well, this is Beep in an epic space emergency: BOUNCE, BOUNCE, BOUNCE, *SHRIEK*.

BOUNCE, BOUNCE, BOUNCE, *SHRIEK*.

BOUNCE, BOUNCE, BOUNCE, *SHRIEK*.

Not super helpful.

I called his name: "'Eepth!"

I called for help: "'Elpth!"

He kept bouncing. I was doomed! And I was going to be known galaxy-wide as "The Kid Who Licked Pluto."

If only I had an Emergency Space Pack.

And that's when it hit me: I did!

I slipped it off and fumbled for the pocket labeled UNIVERSAL INTERSTELLAR DISTRESS SIGNAL BEACON DEVICE. Thank the stars! I pulled it out.

It was a whistle.

Okay, not to worry. Surely there had to be *some-thing* in the Emergency Space Pack I could use. I

dumped all the contents
onto the ice. And saw:

—an old Galaxy Scout
Compass

—three smiley face
Band-Aids

—a bottle of that fizzy,
stingy wound-
cleaning stuff

—a Temporary Shrink Ray

—a Temporary Giganticizer Ray

—a mini pack of Kleenex

—a mini hot water bottle

—a number 2 pencil

—a sewing kit

—an extra space suit button, and

—a Self-Destruct Button

Wait. Self-Destruct Button? Who put *that* there?!

I turned to Beep one last time. It was up to him now. Maybe, just maybe, if he put his little alien mind to it, he could combine all those useless emergency items to build some kind of super communication device that could . . .

BOUNCE, BOUNCE, BOUNCE, *SHRIEK*.

BOUNCE, BOUNCE, BOUNCE, *SHRIEK*.

BOUNCE, BOUNCE, BOUNCE, *SHRIEK*.

Okay, so I really *was* doomed.

"Bob-mother! Bob-mother!" he said. "They come! They come!"

And that's when I understood: Beep had been calling for help the whole time!

"We're coming, we're coming!" a voice called.

"Hey, it's Bob," Atom said, poking his head into the crater.

I was saved!

"And he's . . . oh, man, Blaster, get over here. Wait till you see this!"

Or not.

Out of the corner of my eye, I could see a crowd gathering at the crater's rim.

"'Elpth?" I squeaked.

"Everyone, move back, move back!" Blaster said. "We only have moments to act!" So maybe Blaster had a good side after all.

Then a camera flashed. "Got it!" Blaster said. "Priceless! This is so going on my splog."

Or not.

I began to feel woozy. Just then Beep bounced into view, yelling, "Free Bob-mother! Free Bob-mother!"

"You're his partner," Blaster said. "Why don't *you* free him?"

Beep only repeated, "Free Bob-mother! Free Bob-mother!"

Blaster sighed. "Fine, you little space-troll. But he's stuck pretty bad. There's only one thing we can do now. And that's to"—he paused dramatically—"use the Force."

Of course, the Force! With the Force you could do anything. As long as you were some kind of thousand-year-old master, that is.

Suddenly, two giant arms wrapped around me. Blaster's. And before I could stop him, he began to pull me free. With all *the force* he could muster.

"Gaaaaaaaaaaaaaaaaaaaaaaaaaaaaaaaaaaaaaaaaaaaa aaaaaaaaaaah!" I screamed, nearly fainting from the pain in my tongue.

"Stop!" someone called. "What are you doing?" It sounded like Lani.

"Just trying to help," Blaster said.

"Yeah, right," Lani said, rushing down and pushing him off. "If you really wanted to help, you'd be using your Emergency Space Pack."

Blaster made a face. "The stuff in those is useless," he said. I kind of had to agree.

"Boys," Lani muttered. She grabbed the mini hot water bottle, punctured it with the pencil, and poured the hot water onto my tongue. Instantly, I stumbled back, free.

Why hadn't *I* thought of that?

Beep jumped over and hugged me. "Lani-friend save Bob-mother! Bob-mother owe life!"

Lani folded her arms. "What were you doing anyway? You could have been iced."

I tried to explain, but my numb, sore tongue made it difficult: "Luh luh uh luh uh luh."

"I don't understand."

I pointed to Beep. "Luh luh uh luh!"

Beep immediately began slurping the ground.
"Yum yum orange-swirl!" he said.

Lani smiled. "Aw, isn't Beep cute."

And that was my field trip to Pluto.

SPLOG ENTRY #5:
LUH!

The rest of the trip was fairly uneventful. When we got back to school that afternoon, Professor Zoome called the school nurse, then told me to float straight to the health office.

"Luh!" I said. That translates to: "But I don't *want* to go to the health office. Nurse Lance is scary, and he always tries to give you a *shot*, even when you just have a laser-skinned knee, and anyway, my tongue doesn't hurt *that* bad anymore, I'm sure I'll be able to talk again in about eight or ten light-years." (Though, are light-years time or *distance*? I always forget.)

Professor Zoome pointed. "Feel better."

Beep, of course, tagged along. "Beep sorry Bob-mother dying. Beep have Bob-mother comics when Bob-mother gone?"

"Luh luh!" Beep wasn't *touching* my vintage twenty-first-century comics!

Nurse Lance was waiting for me. "Have a seat," he said, and I floated into the cold metal chair. He strapped me in. "Okay, so are you the student who needs ten space-sickness booster shots or the one who requires a painless, soothing, healing spray to the tongue?"

I opened my mouth wide and pointed with both hands, so he'd be sure to get it. "Luh!"

"Got it," he said. He began preparing a foot-long needle.

"So would you prefer all ten shots on one cheek? Or five on each?"

"LUHHHHHHH!" I screamed. Which cheeks was he talking about anyway?

He pointed the needle at my bottom. "Good

choice. Now, hold still. This will definitely sting. But if you don't pass out, you can have a lollipop. I have raspberry or orange-swirl. Do you have a favorite?"

Beep clapped. "Orange-swirl! Orange-swirl!"

Nurse Lance saw Beep's orange tongue. "Ah, so you must be the one who injured his tongue on Pluto."

"Beep no hurt tongue," Beep said. "Only get brain freeze from lick ice."

Luckily, I remembered my splog writing pad was clipped to my side. I quickly snapped it off and wrote: *NO SHOTS! I AM THE ONE WITH THE HURT TONGUE! ME! ME!*

Nurse Lance squinted. "Oh. So you are. Whyever didn't you say?" He put down the needle—whew!— and showed me two small spray bottles. "Would you like your painless, soothing, healing spray in lemon or lime flavor?"

Beep bounced. "Orange-swirl! Orange-swirl!"

Nurse Lance scowled. "It only comes in lemon or lime."

I pointed. "Luh."

"Lemon. Excellent choice. Open."

I did. *Squirt.* In a second it was over. And he was right. It was painless and soothing, if disgusting.

"I can talk!" I said.

Nurse Lance released me from the chair. "Works every time." He turned to Beep. "As for you: Let's see what we can do about that brain freeze."

Beep clapped. "More ice pop!"

Nurse Lance shook his head. "Not until you get your treatment." He rummaged around and pulled out a spray bottle that said FREEZE B GONE (TO WARM YOUR CHILLY BRAIN). "Ah, knew I had it somewhere. Specially formulated for aliens *only*. One squirt of this on your head, and you can eat all the ice pops you want."

Nurse Lance handed Beep the bottle, and Beep turned and squirted it. On *me*!

"Ow, Beep! That stings! You got it in my eyes!"

Nurse Lance grabbed the bottle back. "What are you doing? I said this formula is meant for *aliens*."

Beep pointed at me. "Alien."

"I'm not the alien, Beep. You are!"

"*BEEP* alien?"

"It tingles," I said as I tried to wipe the rest of the spray off my head.

"Oh, it's probably just seeping into your brain," Nurse Lance said. "On the bright side, the side effects should be only temporary."

"Wait, side effects? What side effects?" I said.

Nurse Lance shrugged. "Beats me. It's never been

administered to a human before." He reached for a needle. "If you're worried, I can easily sedate you."

I backed away. "I'm fine, I'm fine! C'mon, Beep, let's get out of here."

Dazed, I floated out the door. Could this day get any worse?

And that's when I saw the one thing you never, *ever* want to see while you're floating through the hall of a space school: the thin wall between me and space had suddenly disappeared!

The day was officially worse.

SPLOG ENTRY #6:
New and Improved

Beep, look!" I yelled. "We're doomed!"

Beep turned. "Doomed?"

I pointed. "The wall—it's gone! We're about to be sucked into space!"

"Yay!" Beep said.

"Not yay!" I said. But it wasn't too late for action. So I did the one sensible thing I could think of: put my hands over my eyes and screamed!

"Gahhhhhh!" I said. "I can see my own bones!" I lowered my hands. "And I can see inside you, too!"

Beep blushed. "Inside Beep?"

His stomach held a horrible mixture of melted ice and pencils and hot fudge and my favorite red sock I'd been missing since yesterday and . . .

"Beep, did you eat my sock?"

He tried to cover himself. "Sock? Who sock?"

I pointed. "The one right there."

"How Bob-mother see?"

I blinked. "I don't know." And that's when it hit me: "I have X-ray vision! It must be a side effect from that stuff getting in my eyes."

Beep shook his head. "Poor Bob-mother."

I looked through my hand again. "Actually, it's pretty cool. I can see my distal phalanx. My first metacarpal. My scaphoid!"

"Bob-mother make funny names too."

"Those are names of bones, Beep," I explained.

"Bob-mother smart."

"Whoa, Beep. You're right." I could feel a warm tingling all through my head. "The medicine is also affecting my left prefrontal cortex!"

"Huh?"

I grabbed Beep by the shoulders. "This is incredible, Beep. For the first time in my life I actually feel smart. Discerning. Knowledgeable. Sagacious!"

Beep shook his head. "Not self."

"Exactly! It's overriding my fear receptors too. I feel . . . I feel brave!"

Beep clapped. "Very not self!"

"It's amazing, Beep, my chum!"

"What chum?" asked Beep.

"Friend. Comrade. Acquaintance. Pal."

He smiled. "Beep chum!"

"Hurry, let's get back to class. With any luck, Professor Zoome will be giving us a big test!"

We returned just as Lani was finishing her report on our trip.

" . . . and in conclusion," she said, "my pet—I mean *subject*—spiders, Alpha, Beta, and Zilly, enjoyed the trip very much. Or, in their own words . . ." Smiling, she then pulled out a jar, in which the spiders had written in their webs:

Her smile faded. "Some planet," she whispered to Zilly. "You were supposed to write some *planet*."

Zilly scampered sadly down her web. I grabbed the jar and studied her closely.

"It's understandable that Zilly is distracted," I pointed out. "After all, she's carrying 2,128 eggs inside her, which will one day hatch into 2,128 hypercute spiders."

Beep looked at Zilly and clapped. "Spider-mommy!"

Lani's mouth dropped open. "How do you know that, Bob?"

"Um . . . just a guess." I was now smart enough not to advertise my amazing new abilities.

Blaster stepped forward. "Looks like Bob thinks he has *X-ray vision*. Just like LunaGirl!" LunaGirl is a very popular cartoon character of our time. At least with five-year-olds.

I winced as I looked at him. "I thought you liked LunaGirl."

"No way," Blaster said. "She's for girls."

I leaned over to Beep and whispered, "Then why is he wearing LunaGirl underpants?"

Beep clapped. "Bob-mother funny!"

Professor Zoome cleared her throat. "If we could please end our discussions, I'd like everyone to clear their desks. It's time for a big test."

"Yes!" I whispered.

Zenith raised her hand. "What's the test on?"

"Black holes."

"But we haven't even learned about black holes!" said Zenith.

"Of course you haven't," the professor said. "The literature about black holes is unbearably confusing."

Kids started to grumble. How could she test us on something we hadn't studied?

I raised my hand. "What if we actually visited one?"

The room became silent.

"Go on, Bob," she said.

"There's a super massive black hole at the center of the galaxy. It would be a great learning opportunity. As long as we aren't sucked in and crushed into micro-atoms, that is."

I looked around the room. All my classmates seemed terrified. Even Blaster looked faint.

But Professor Zoome clasped her hands and beamed. "Exactly what I was going to propose! Kids, bring an extra-yummy lunch tomorrow for the trip. It may be your last. Class dismissed."

SPLOG ENTRY #7:
Back to (Sigh) Normal

Beep and I made our way toward the dorms. For once, life was looking up. I was smart. I was brave. And because of me, we were actually going to experience the deadliest wonder of nature!

Beep tugged on my sleeve. "Bob-mother? Beep have big question."

"Go ahead, Beep. Ask me anything! The speed

of light. The composition of Saturn's rings. The number of atoms in the universe!"

"What color Beep sock?"

I glanced at his bare feet. "That's your big question?"

He rubbed his tummy. "Beep eat more sock. Fun game."

I sighed. "If you insist." I looked into his tummy. At least, I tried to.

"Well?" Beep said.

"Hmm, let me try again." I squinted. Hard. I could see an inch in, maybe two, but even that was getting difficult.

"Oh no," I said. "The side effects of the spray must be wearing off!"

"Power go bye," Beep said.

I feared he was right. "Let's get back to our room. Quick!"

Before we could move, Lani swooped in. "Hey. I've been looking for you."

"I'm kind of in a hurry," I said.

"And I'm kind of worried," she said. "And not just me, the entire class. No one's ever been to a black hole before. Do you even know what they're like?"

"Well," I said. "By studying the quantum theory of curved space-time, one can deduct that black holes are very, um . . ."

"Dangerous? Hazardous?"

I struggled. "Very, um, very, um . . ."

"Deadly?"

Did she have to keep saying those things? "I meant to say very . . . black."

Beep shook his head. "Sock not black, it *blue*."

Lani looked at me in disbelief. "What's going on with you, Bob?"

I faked a smile. "Nothing. Never been better."

"Anyway, all I'm asking," she said, "is if you know what you've gotten us into?"

"I'd much rather go on a hayride!" I blurted out.

Lani gave me another strange look. "Are you *sure* you're okay, Bob?"

"Uh . . . Uh . . ."

Now that I was my normal self again, my worst fears washed over me. Heights, check. Darkness, check. Space, check. Death, check.

Black holes had them all.

"Gaaaaaaaaaaaaaaaaaaaaaaaaaaaaaaah!" I screamed, rushing away.

I was doomed. I was doomed!!

I raced by my classmate Hadron, who was holding his bare foot. "Has anyone seen my blue sock?"

Doomed.

SPLOG ENTRY #8:
The Best of Plans, the Worst of Plans

I lay in bed that night going over possible solutions with Beep, who had the top bunk in our quarters.

"I can pretend to be sick," I said.

"Plan good!" said Beep.

"Of course, then Nurse Lance will insist on giving me a shot."

"Plan bad."

"I know! I'll suggest an even better destination!

We can go to the moon of Mars, the one that has that new candy factory. Everyone likes candy factories."

"Plan good!" said Beep.

"But that's where they take all the kindergarteners. Professor Zoome would never agree."

"Plan bad."

"How about I steal the Astrobus, travel to the outer rings of Saturn, and hide there?"

"Plan good!" said Beep.

"But I don't know how to fly."

"Plan bad."

I thought and thought and thought. Then I dozed a little. Then Beep and I read some comics. Then I dozed some more. Then Beep's snoring woke me up (not to gross you out, but he snores from his *bottom*, if you know what I mean).

I sprang up so hard I came out of my bed-straps

and floated into the middle of the room.

"I got it!" I said.

Beep's eyes popped open. "Plan good?"

"Very good. My problem isn't the black hole. It's my personality! We have to go back to the health office and snatch that bottle of Freeze B Gone. To make me smart and brave again."

"Plan good! Plan good!"

"And when I say *we* I mean *you*."

"Plan bad! Plan bad!"

"No, Beep, it's logical: The spray cures my fears. But I'm scared of Nurse Lance. So I can't get the spray unless I've already *had* the spray."

Beep nodded. "Logic good."

"Plus"—I floated closer to put on the charm—"if you do a good job I just might have an orange-swirl ice pop waiting with your name on it."

"Why Beep want name on it?"

"In *sprinkles*."

"Ooooooooh," Beep said, his face brightening. "Sprinkles good."

"Great." I landed back in bed. "Now let's get some rest. We're going to need it."

The next morning, no one in class seemed very happy. Probably because, thanks to me, we were about to head on a journey with little hope of return.

On the other hand, our lunches were extra yummy.

The second that attendance was done, I raised my hand. "Professor Zoome?"

"Yes, Bob?"

"Before we go, can I take Beep to the health office?"

"Is something wrong?" she asked.

I leaned forward and lowered my voice. "Well, uh, Beep likes to sleep on the bus, and, um, he's been *snoring* a lot lately. Don't want to, you know, stink up the place too bad."

She lifted an eyebrow. "Hurry back."

"We will."

I led Beep to the health room door. "You remember what to do?" I whispered.

He nodded.

"Then go," I said, pushing him inside. I ducked down behind the door to eavesdrop.

"Well, hello there, little one," I heard Nurse Lance say. "What kind of shot may I be giving you today?"

"No shot. Beep swallow sock."

"Ah, I see. So it's surgery you require. I'll get my laser."

"No. Beep want *more* sock."

"But I don't have more socks. Only the ones I'm wearing."

"Look good to Beep."

"Hands off!"

"Beep sad with no sock."

"Here, you can have a bandage roll."

"Yum!" Beep said.

"You weren't supposed to eat it!"

"More?"

"No more!"

"Pencil?"

"Certainly not."

"Cottony ball?"

"Leave those alone!"

"Squirt bottle?"

"Don't open that!" Nurse Lance said. "That's the medicine cabinet!"

I heard crashing. "Oop," Beep said. "Beep sorry. Beep help clean."

"You've been enough help already. Just get out!"

"But Beep want more."

"I said, out!" Nurse Lance yelled.

"Bye!" Beep said as he drifted out.

"And stay out!" As the door slid shut, I heard Nurse Lance's muffled voice add, "Hey, where's my sock?"

I pulled Beep around the corner. "Did you get the spray?" I asked.

He smiled wide.

"Beep, you're my hero!" I glanced at his empty hands. "Uh, where is it?"

"Safe place!"

"Behind your back?" I asked.

"Back no safe, silly Bob-mother."

My heart began to sink. "In your ear, maybe?"

"No in ear!" he said. "That tickle."

I gulped. I didn't want to know. I really didn't. "Safe where, Beep?"

Beep patted his tummy. "Bottle yum!"

SPLOG ENTRY #9
A Tale of Two Tummies

I wanted to be mad at Beep, but he'd done exactly what I'd asked. The problem was, I didn't have a plan B. Or C, or D, or even Z to the 10th power.

All I had was a yummy lunch (jelly but no peanut butter, yes!).

As we floated back to class, we ran into Professor Zoome, who was already leading the others down the hall. "Beep and Bob!" she called. "The Astrobus is leaving in two minutes!"

"But—" I began.

"No buts. We're on a tight schedule."

Suddenly, I had a plan B. "But my lunchbox is in the classroom. I have to go back and get it!"

"No time," she said, dragging me along. "You can have half of my peanut butter sandwich."

"I'm allergic to peanut butter," I said.

"Then you'll just have to hope they have a food court."

"By a black hole?"

"You never know," Professor Zoome replied.

Beep clapped. "Food court!"

I slapped my forehead.

Moments later Beep and I were aboard the bus,

watching a trail of kids slink by us, one by one. It was as if we were invisible. No one wanted to come near us.

"No one like Beep?" Beep asked, his eyes wide with hurt.

"No, Beep. They don't like *me*," I said, looking at the floor.

"Hey, Bob," I heard a voice say. "Mind if we sit here?"

I looked up at Lani and smiled. "Sure."

"Sure you mind or sure we can?"

"Lani sit next to Beep and Bob-mother!" Beep answered.

Unfortunately, Lani clutched her jar of those icky crawly things. Did she have to bring that everywhere?

As it took off, the Astrobus shook, stirred, pushed,

pulled, stretched, and flattened every atom in my body. We swung a hard left at Neptune. And my stomach swung a hard right.

As we passed Pluto, Beep said, "Where ice pop Bob-mother promise?"

How could he even think of eating at a time like this? "Aren't you full of socks?"

"Socks not in *eat*ing tummy."

I looked at him.

"Socks in *pouch* tummy!" To my shock, he reached into a pocket of skin on his front and pulled out a red sock.

"Whoa!" I said. "I didn't know you could do that."

Beep pointed into his mouth. "Go down right side, go to eating tummy. Go down left, go to pouch tummy. Then Beep reach in pouch to take back out."

"I wondered where you always stored stuff," I said.

He patted himself and belched. "Beep pretty full. See, here blue sock," he said, pulling more stuff out of his pouch. "And bandage roll. And green sock. And medicine spray. And yellow sock. And pencil. And—"

"Wait, medicine spray? That's the Freeze B Gone!" I grabbed it before he could swallow it again. "Beep, I could kiss you!" Okay, maybe not kiss. But I did lean over to hug the little guy. Which probably would have been nicer if my arm hadn't gotten stuck in his pouch.

"Tee-hee, tickle!" Beep said.

"Gross! *Gross!*" I said. "Stop squirming, Beep, so I can get it out!"

"Beep tickle! Beep tickle!" he laughed, squirming even more.

Sadly, it went on like that for a while. By the time I finally got free—and Beep stopped giggling—the bus was quiet. Everyone was gaping out the window.

With a growing sense of dread, I turned. "Oh . . . oh no."

Beep peered out too. "Beep no see nothing." He wiped the glass. "Just black."

"Exactly," I whispered. We were there.

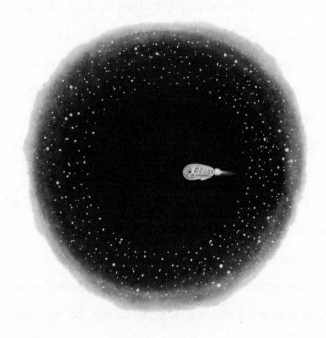

SPLOG ENTRY #10:
Testing, Testing

Warning: I'm about to write a graphic, horrifying splog entry that you might want to skip if you're sensitive to those kinds of things. Sorry, but the part coming up is about to get a bit—last chance to bail, I really did warn you—*educational*.

That's right: As we were all staring into the vast hole in space that was deeper and blacker and more mind crushingly terrifying than anything I'd ever imagined, Professor Zoome decided to give a *lecture*.

"Black holes," she began, "are defined as regions of space-time formed by the death and collapse of very large stars, resulting in compact, dark masses with such strong gravitational fields that nothing that gets caught in their pull—including matter, light, or money—has any hope of ever coming back out. Any questions?"

Hands went up.

"Yes, Comet?"

"Will this be on the test?"

"If you survive, yes."

More hands went up.

"Hadron?" Professor Zoome said.

"What if we *don't* survive?"

"A zero will be averaged into your final grade. Zenith, you have a question?"

"What if we're only injured?" Zenith asked.

"Injuries by black hole are not possible. Once you pass even a micrometer beyond the point known as the 'event horizon'—or *bye-bye forever zone*—you will be stretched into an infinite strand of subatomic spaghetti."

Beep raised his hand. "Ooo, ooo!"

"Yes, Beep?"

"Spaghetti yum!"

"That was not a question. My informational talk is now concluded. Please suit up so you can go outside. Who would like to be first in the air lock?"

Before I knew what was happening, a hand grabbed my arm from behind and thrust it into the air. "Me, me!" Blaster said, mimicking my voice.

Professor Zoome smiled. "Very brave of you, Bob. Once again, very brave, indeed."

SPLOG ENTRY #11
Spaced Out

As I was suiting up, Professor Zoome went over the rules.

"Once you're outside, class, you'll be connected to the bus by a thin rope that attaches to your Emergency Space Pack. Whatever you do, don't push the Quick Release Switch, which is right next to the Self-Destruct Button."

Who designed these things?!

"Please stay with your partner and record as many observations of the black hole as you can. Extra credit to the student who goes closest to the bye-bye forev—er, *event horizon*—without being sucked inside." She looked at me. "Ready?"

"Al—almost," I stammered. "Just have to, uh, tie my shoe."

"Space boots don't have laces," she pointed out.

"They don't?" I said, kneeling anyway. Then, when I was sure no one was looking, I lifted the spray bottle of Freeze B Gone and doused it all over my head.

"Ready now?" Professor Zoome said.

"Coming. Just need my helmet and I'm set." I grabbed it from the seat, but somehow it didn't feel right. "Wait, this isn't my helmet," I said. "This is a jar of . . . gaaaaaaaaaaaaaaaaaaaaaaaaaaaaaaaaaaaah!"

Lani grabbed the jar of spiders away. "That's not funny. You're scaring them!" She peered inside. "It's okay, Alpha. Don't tremble, Beta. Hey, where's Zilly? Zilly?"

Behind her, Blaster laughed. Well, *some*one thought it was funny.

The spray's side effects must have been kicking in, because I squinted at Blaster and bravely said, "You're a mean bully, you know?"

He held up his hands. "I was just kidding."

"Yeah, sure," I replied.

He suddenly got all serious. "Really. I'm sorry." He held up my actual helmet. "Here, no more jokes, okay?"

I took the helmet. "I guess."

He held out his hand. "We sporky?"

Sporky was *my* word. But I wanted to be a good sport, so I shook. "Sporky."

Next to me, Beep was trembling. "No sporky! No sporky!"

"It's okay, Beep," I told him. "I'm fine now that I have this bottle of . . . Wait, what's this?" For the first time, I read the bottle closely. "Beep, this isn't for brain freeze. It's for *fleas.* You got the wrong spray!"

"Bob-mother no have fleas," Beep said. "It work!"

"Oh no. Oh no."

"Time to go, Bob," Professor Zoome said. "But please don't forget to put your helmet on."

"But . . ."

"Now into the air lock."

"But . . ."

"Attach the thin space rope."

"BUT . . . !"

She pushed a button, thrusting me into raw space, and waved.

"Have fun!"

SPLOG ENTRY #12:
Point Break

Okay, so there I was: my darkest hour. Just me, space, and the gaping mouth of a super massive black hole.

But you know what? As bad as life gets (and it gets pretty bad!), there's one thing that can always make it better: a faithful field trip partner by your side.

That's right: a faithful field trip partner. Right by your . . .

I turned left. "Beep?"

I turned right. *"Beep?"*

I spun around. "BEEP?"

Beep waved from *inside* the safe, warm Astrobus!

"BEEP, GET OUT HERE!" I screamed.

Within seconds the bus door opened and he shot out to join me.

"No worry," he said, holding up his thin cord. "Beep bring space rope."

"Did you remember to hook it to the ship?"

His cheeks reddened. "Oop."

"Beep, hold on!" I grabbed on to him before he floated away.

Beep turned toward the vast swirl of infinite darkness. "View nice. Beep draw."

"It's just *black*," I said.

Beep nodded. "Easy that way."

I struggled to keep my grip firm as Beep rummaged in his pouch for his drawing supplies. But my gloves were thick, and I didn't know if I could hold on to Beep for much longer. At least things couldn't get worse.

Then I heard a snap.

"BEEP!" I yelled. "Our space rope just snapped! We're doomed!"

"Doomed!" he yelled back.

"Doomed!" I yelled.

"Doomed!"

"Doomed!"

"Doomed!" I yelled. Or was that him? I was losing track.

Then I just started to scream. "Gaaaaaaaaaaaa-aaaaaaaahhhh!"

"Gaaaaaaaaaaaaaaaaaaaahhhh!" Beep screamed back.

"Gaaaaaaaaaaaaaaaaaaaahhhh!" I screamed.

"Gaaaaaaaaaaaaaaaaaaaahhhh!"

"Gaaaaaaaaaaaaaaaaaaaahhhh!"

"Gaaaaaaaaaaaaaaaa—wait, who scream now?" Beep said.

"You!"

"Why Beep scream?"

"Our space rope snapped!"

He tugged the taut rope. "Rope no snap."

"It didn't?"

He shook his head sadly. "No. More worse."

"What could possibly be worse than our space rope snapping?!"

He held up his pencil. "Point break."

The pencil point? That was *it*? I wanted to strangle him. But before I could, a voice came on in my helmet: "Professor Zoome here. Bob, are you alive?"

"I think so," I squeaked.

"Good," she answered. "Because the rest of us are suited up and ready to come out. We're just awaiting your word."

That was easy: "*HELP!!!*"

"An odd word for the occasion," she said. "But a word all the same. We'll be right out."

"*LET ME BACK IN! PLEASE LET ME IN!*"

"I only asked for one word, Bob. Please follow directions. Professor Zoome out."

SPLOG ENTRY #13:
Lost and Found

One at a time, students left the bus. Before I could say *Silvery spaceships speed by sparkly stars* five times fast, the entire class was dangling outside at the end of their own very thin space ropes. Beep still held on to mine.

Hadron pointed his camera at the black hole and snapped a few shots, then frowned at the results. "Guess I forgot to turn on the flash."

Professor Zoome smiled at the black hole. "Isn't it simply singular?" At least *she* was having a good time.

Zenith floated up to me. "Hi, cutey," she said.

I reddened. "Uh . . ."

"Not you!" she said. "Beep!"

Beep floated upside down. "Beep cutey! Beep cutey!"

I glanced around. "Where's Lani? Isn't she with you?"

"She's still in the Astrobus," Zenith said. "She lost something important, and she's looking for it."

"C'mon, Beep," I said, aiming us toward the bus window. Sure enough, Lani was floating up and down the aisle, looking under every seat. I knocked on the glass. "Zenith said you lost something," I called. "Can I come in and help you look?"

She faked a weak smile. "That would be great."

"What'd you lose? Your notebook? Your helmet?" I glanced at Beep. "Your *sock*?"

"A zillion times worse!" she cried.

"Your lunch?" I guessed.

She held up that awful jar. "I thought Zilly was hiding, but she must have gotten out! Where could she be? I'll die if she's lost!"

I recoiled. "Well, gee, I hope you find it," I said.

"You're not going to come in and help?" she said.

"It's just that I, you know, have this black hole to explore, and I kind of need all the extra credit I can get, and . . ."

I stopped at the eerie sound of laughter by my side. It was a laugh I knew well.

Blaster's.

I slowly turned. It was Blaster, all right.

"Looking for something?" he said, smothering another chuckle.

Beep tugged on my arm.

"Not me," I said. "Lani. She lost her"—I didn't even want to say it—"arthropod, or whatever you call it."

"Spidey," Beep said.

"Spid-*er*," I corrected him.

"No!" Beep said, pointing wildly at my forehead. "Spidey! *Spidey!*"

Inside the bus, Lani smiled and let out a huge sigh. "Bob, there she is! What a relief. She's been with you the whole time!"

And that's when I felt the light movement on my skin and realized that of all the infinite spots in all of infinite space in all the infinite universes, Lani's creepy spider happened to be in the worst spot imaginable:

MY HELMET!!!!!!!!

!!

SPLOG ENTRY #14:
Bye-Bye Zone

'd like to say that I then found the courage to let the awful, hairy, disgusting creature continue to crawl over me long enough to make it back inside the Astrobus.

But I didn't.

Instead, I clawed at my visor.

And opened it up.

The spider whooshed right out.

Luckily, before all my oxygen could whoosh out with it, I slapped my visor back down.

I sucked in a deep breath. "Whew, that was close, Beep. Unlike you, we Earth beings need to breathe."

He pointed to a little speck in the distance. "Like spidey?"

I watched it float away.

Yes. Like spidey.

"Bob!" Lani called. "Do something!"

I turned to tell her it was too late. And anyway, it was just a spider. But then I saw Lani's face pressed to the window—sad and scared and helpless. Even if she suited up in record time, she would never make it out before her favorite—but, for the record, *disgusting*—pet was sucked toward certain doom. (Along with its 2,128 unborn awful little babies.)

And it was all my fault.

"Bob, please," she pleaded one last time.

I spun toward the others. "Catch it!" I called. "Someone catch that gross little thing!"

Zenith swiped for it. But missed. Flash was speedy. But he missed too.

Hadron was still trying to figure out why his pictures came out so dark.

Professor Zoome zoomed, but even she was too late. The spider was now past the longest space rope. A few thousand more feet and it would be sucked into darkness forever.

Beep tapped my shoulder. "Spidey have to go bye?" he asked. "Like Beep get lost and go bye from Beep family?" Did he really have to tug on my heartstrings like that?

I faced the black hole. Which was certain death.

Then I faced the bus. And Lani.

Then the black hole again. Did I dare attempt the impossible? Without the spray? Could I find my courage after all?

"Oh, *now* I get it," Hadron said, holding up his camera. "I left the *lens* cap on."

SPLOG ENTRY #15:
BIG Trouble

So let's see, what horrible thing happened next? Oh yeah: My space rope tautened and I couldn't go any farther. Even though the rope was my only lifeline to the bus, I reached down and hit the Quick Release Switch. With a click, the rope came free.

Beep was still clinging to me, so I brushed him

free. "Get back to the bus, Beep. Before the strong pull of the black hole sucks you in!"

"Where Bob-mother go?!"

I aimed for the black hole. "I have a plan, Beep."

"Good plan?"

I shrugged. "Probably not."

Before I could stop him, Beep zoomed after me and grabbed on. "Then Beep come too!"

A small part of me wanted to argue with him. But the bigger part was glad he was there.

"Keep your eyes on the spider," I said. Ahead of us, it flailed its little legs. I wondered how much longer it could survive.

"This fun!" Beep said, waving his sketchbook. "Beep draw."

"Beep, this way!" I flew forward, hand extended. The spider seemed to be slowing down. All I had to do now was to carefully reach out, put my hand around its disgusting little body, and . . .

"Got it!"

In front of us, the black hole loomed larger.

"Now what Bob-mother do?"

That was a very good question.

I yanked off my Emergency Space Pack. "There's one last part of my plan, Beep. But I can't make any promises." I pulled out item after item—whistle, Kleenex, sewing kit—and tossed them away. "It has to be in here somewhere."

Beep caught the items with his mouth. "Yum!"

"Here it is!" I said, but it turned out to be the number 2 pencil.

Beep scowled. "No time for draw, Bob-mother."

No kidding! Panicked, I kept searching until, finally, I found it: the Temporary Giganticizer Ray!

Beep clapped. "Make Beep big! Make Beep big! Make Beegib!" Another tongue twister.

"Not you," I said, pointing the ray at the only target that could save us now. "Zilly."

I pushed the button before I could change my mind. In a quick, terrible instant, the inch-long webcrawler in my hand ballooned up to the size of an asteroid. To my infinite horror, I could now count each bristling hair on its slimy body and catch the gleam on the end of each sharp fang.

"Gahhhhhhhhhhhhhhhh!" I said, grasping on to a leg the size of a tree.

"This Bob-mother good plan?" Beep asked.

"Now, Zilly!" I called. "Shoot your web! Shoot it right at the bus!"

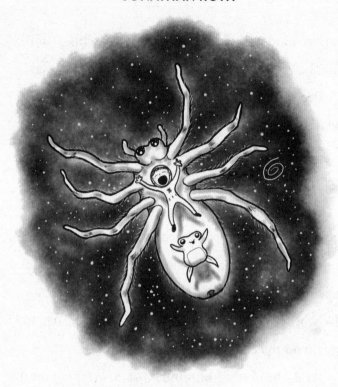

The spider stared at me with multiple rows of gigantic glass eyeballs. They reflected the bus on one side and complete blackness on the other. We whooshed faster and faster as the giant force of nature pulled us in. We were seconds from being stretched into spaghetti and swallowed whole.

"You do understand, Zilly, right?" I said. "It's all up to you now!"

To my horror, the spider then turned to face the black hole straight on.

"Other way, *other way*!" I screamed.

But Zilly didn't budge. She was going in headfirst, and taking us with her.

"Listen, I'm sorry if I offended you, Zilly. Spiders just creep me out, that's all. Nothing personal, right?"

Still nothing. We were doomed.

"Sorry, Beep," I said. "Plan bad. Plan very, very bad."

I closed my eyes and waited for the end.

SPLOG ENTRY #16:
Radiant

S peaking of ends, if I'd ever bothered to actually *learn* about spiders, I would have known that most species shoot their webs from spinnerets—yucky things located on their *bottoms*.

Zilly wasn't turning to face the black hole, she was aiming her web-shooters at the bus.

Good thing too, because about one second from

the point of no return, Zilly shot her webs—*thwap, thwap*—and we were saved.

"Beep says yay!" said Beep.

"Yay!" I yelled.

"Kk-kk!" said Zilly.

Except that—just our luck—the web *missed the bus!*

"Beep says oh no!" said Beep.

"Oh no!" I yelled.

"Kk-kk!" said Zilly.

But then I realized that Zilly's web had stuck to something else: Blaster's helmet! And since he was attached to the bus by his rope, we were now attached too.

"Beep says yay!" said Beep.

"Yay!" I yelled.

"Kk-kk!" said Zilly.

Zilly reeled us in, a split second before the Temporary

Giganticizer Ray wore off. I tumbled through the air lock door as Zilly shrank back to normal size.

"Are you all alive?!" Professor Zoome asked when we were inside.

"I think so," I said. To my side, Blaster scraped web strands off his visor.

Professor Zoome reached around to give me a single pat. "You've earned a passing grade indeed."

Lani was waiting with her jar. "Zilly!" she cried, hugging the small spider.

"Beep hug too?" Beep asked.

"Absolutely," Lani said, hugging him, too.

Then she floated before me. Was I going to get a hug too? Not that I wanted one, because I don't really go for those kinds of things, especially from girls. I was just an ordinary space explorer, doing what needed to be done. In fact, I . . .

. . . felt the air being squeezed right out of me!

"Lani hug Bob-mother!" Beep said. "Lani hug Bob-mother!"

A bright light flashed. "Yes!" Hadron said as the moment was immortalized on his camera. "Finally."

SPLOG ENTRY #17:
Good Night, Space

Good news! Professor Zoome looked at my splog entries so far and told me I got a perfect grade and six stars of extra credit! She also said she looked forward to seeing me write more about my memorable (but horrible) adventures in space.

To which I said: "You know what? Me too!"

"Beep draw! Beep draw!"

"Yes," I told Beep, "you can still do the drawings."

(Until I can afford to hire a professional, that is.)

"Send time-velope now?" Beep asked.

I had put all the entries from the week into one folder, and the folder into the time-velope. I was about to hit send when I heard a knock on my dorm room door.

It was Lani.

"Oh, hey," I said.

"Hey," she replied. "What are you doing?"

"Sending my splogs."

"Then what?"

I shrugged. "No big plans."

"Great." She brightened. "Because I was thinking: How would you like to go check out a comet with me? Or maybe explore the asteroid belt? Or maybe . . ."

"Actually," I said, "Beep and I thought we'd stay in tonight and read comics. It's been a long week. Very long."

"Oh." She bit her lip and floated toward the door.

"You can, you know, join us if you want," I added quickly.

"Lani stay! Lani stay!"

She eyed my vintage collection. "Aren't comics for *little* kids?" she asked.

"Comics are for *everyone*. Here, check one out." I tossed her a title, believe it or not, called *Spider-Man*. I think it was about some awful, evil supervillain. I sure wasn't about to look at it.

She grinned at the cover. "Thanks," she said, her voice bright. "This does look fun."

"Comics, yay!" That was Beep, not me.

"Speaking of spiders," she said, "Alpha, Beta, and Zilly wrote some new things in their webs today. Want to see?"

She'd brought *spiders* to my room?! No offense, but

even though I owed my life to one, spiders still made me cringe.

I gulped. "I guess."

She opened her pack and pulled out the jar. "I think you'll like it," she said.

I got closer. And peered inside.

Alpha's web said $ax^2 + bx + c = 0$. Beta's said *Pi r squared*.

And then there was Zilly's. It said:

I couldn't help but smile. "And you're pretty sporky for a spider, Zilly."

"And Beep!"

"And Beep, too."

And so we curled up with our comics, ate some orange-swirl ice pops, and had a pretty good evening in space.

SEND

Bob's Extra-Credit Fun Space Facts! (Even though nothing is fun about space!)

Pluto was first discovered in 1930 by some guy named **Clyde Tombaugh**. But since it's so small and so far from Earth, not even the biggest telescopes could tell if it was blue or green or yellow like Pluto the cartoon dog. But then the *New Horizons* space probe flew by in 2015, and people everywhere learned that Pluto is rusty orange with a big white heart! It's not a real heart, of course, just a giant skating rink of frozen **nitrogen**, **methane**, and **carbon monoxide**, whatever those things are. Pluto also has five **moons**, which may seem like a lot, but it can get pretty lonely out there.

Dwarf planet?

Though Pluto was once called a **planet**, it was then demoted to a *dwarf* **planet** for some reason, and the kids of Earth were not happy. Kids like Pluto because it's small and cool. An eleven-year-old girl called **Venetia Burney** even got to give Pluto its name! I don't know what it was called before that. Probably **Dwarfy**.

Pluto *is* pretty cool—in fact it's about **minus 380 degrees**! So if you ever go there, remember to *always* wear your Ice Boots and never, ever, ever, EVER try to lick the ground.

ACKNOWLEDGMENTS

It takes a large ground crew to help even a small book series blast off. My amazing crew includes my stellar agent, Natalie Lakosil; my out-of-this-world editor, Amy Cloud; the planet's best writing partners, Fataima Ahmed and Lauren Francis-Sharma; my long-time mission buddies, Robin Galbraith and Kurtis Scaletta; the indispensable communities of SCBWI, the 2017 Debut Group, the Electric Eighteens, and the entire team at Aladdin; my star-bright

ACKNOWLEDGMENTS

sisters, Catherine and Elizabeth, and bro, Matt; my talented niece Gwen (whose artistry can be found in one of the Astrobus windows); my first and most important teachers: my mom, Karen, and dad, Guy; and the one who truly makes me fly, my dear wife, Lisa Marie. To you all, Beep says YAY!

READ THE NEXT BEEP AND BOB ADVENTURE:

PARTY CRASHERS

SPLOG ENTRY #1:
Star Bores

Dear Kids of the Past,

Hi. My name's Bob and I live and go to school in space. That's right, space. Pretty sporky, huh? I'm the new kid this year at Astro Elementary, the only school in orbit around one of the outer planets. There's just one micro little problem:

SPACE IS STUPENDOUSLY BORING!

I mean, sure, you can spend about two minutes

staring out giant picture windows at the infinite wonders of the universe. But then what? We're so far from Earth, the television reception is terrible. And the only channel that does come in well is—don't say I didn't warn you—*educational*.

Beep just said, "Beep like watch *Star Words*! Learn from robot ABCD-2!" Beep is a young alien who got separated from his 600 siblings when they were playing hide-and-seek in some asteroid field. Then he floated around space for a while, until he ended up here. Sad, huh?

You know what's even sadder? I was the one who found him knocking on our space station's air lock door and let him in. Now he thinks I'm his new mother! But since he also thinks *Star Words* is a good show (even though it's for three-year-olds), you can tell he's a little confused.

But I still like him.

"Beep like Bob-mother, too!"

Beep is pretty good at drawing, so I let him do all the pictures for these space logs (splogs, as we call them) before sending them back in time for you to read. Just don't hold me responsible if he only doodles his favorite *Star Words* alpha-bots.

Anyway, that's my life. Enjoy!

SPLOG ENTRY #2:
Party Invites from Heaven

Okay, I know I just said space was pretty much the most boring thing ever, but that was *before* I had to sit through our class history reports. Each student had to choose a book about a historical event and report back to the class.

After listening to Zenith drone on about the first moon missions, and Blaster share every detail about World War P, I didn't think there was any history *left*. My brain was seconds from shutting down.

"Very good, children," Professor Zoome said when they were done. "Sadly, we don't have time for more today. We will resume on Monday with"—she checked her clipboard—"Bob."

Beep clapped. "Bob-mother, yay!"

Gulp. I wasn't even halfway through the book I'd picked out yet! I leaned toward Beep and whispered, "Luckily, she didn't say *which* Monday."

"And by Monday," she continued, "I mean the day after the day after tomorrow."

Beep clapped again. So much for a nice, quiet weekend staring out the window.

Lani grabbed my arm when I was halfway out the classroom door. Lani (short for Laniakea Supercluster) is my best friend at school who *isn't* a confused alien. Not that I think about her a lot or anything, but "Lani" means "heaven" in Hawaiian. Of course, "Lani" can also mean "sky," depending on—

"Hey, Beep! Hi, Bob! I'm glad I caught you," she said. "Are you doing anything this weekend?"

My face grew hot. "Well . . . ," I began.

"Great!" She pulled out a couple of envelopes. "Because I'm inviting you both to my birthday party!"

Birthday party? I broke into a cold sweat. "There's not going to be a clown, is there?"

She shook her head. "No. Why?"

"My parents hired a clown for my birthday once, and I had to hide in a closet the whole time."

Lani smiled. "No clown, Bob. I promise."

"Whew. But, uh, what about

a magician? Because there was this other incident—"

"No magician either."

"Swell. And no guy in a purple dinosaur suit?"

"Bob, how many traumatic birthdays have you had?"

I counted on both hands. "Pretty much all of them."

"Well, this one's going to be different," she said. "Just be sure to bring a bathing suit."

"You're having a pool party?"

"There's a pool in the water park."

I perked up. "Water park?"

"Actually, where we're going, there are three water parks."

"*Three* water parks?"

"But if those aren't your style, there are also sixteen amusement parks."

"Sixteen amusement parks!"

"Though, if that's too tiring," she said, "I suppose you could stay in your room and surf the twelve million hypershow channels."

I began to drool. "Tw-tw-twelve million?"

"It's a lot, I know," Lani said. "But my parents insisted on having the party on some amazing new star cruiser that's taking a tour around Neptune. I hope you don't mind."

I shook my head. "We can handle it."

"I'm so glad!" Lani said. "We leave tomorrow and get back Sunday night."

Beep pulled on my sleeve. "When Bob-mother do big report?"

I pushed him away. "Silly Beep! He's always

joking." But when Lani was gone, I added, "Don't worry, Beep. I'm sure I can fit in my homework somewhere in between SIXTEEN AWESOME AMUSEMENT PARKS!"

I tore open the invitation. It read:

Lani is having a party!

On the maiden voyage of

the *STARSHIP TITANIC*!

Motto: The 100% Safest Ship in the Galaxy.

100% Guaranteed!

"Hmm, that name sounds familiar," I said, reaching into my backpack for the book I chose for my report (mainly because it was the only history book in graphic novel form I could find). It was about some ship that sailed on Earth a really long time ago (even for you kids of the past).

I read the title: *Titanic: A Night to Remember.*